To Liam and Anouska, with love
from C F

For Lorcan, Mark and Gerry, and, as ever, Tiziana
from J B-B

LITTLE TIGER PRESS
An imprint of Magi Publications
1 The Coda Centre, 189 Munster Road, London SW6 6AW
www.littletigerpress.com

First published in Great Britain 2002

Text © Claire Freedman 2002
Illustrations © John Bendall-Brunello 2002
Claire Freedman and John Bendall-Brunello have asserted their
rights to be identified as the author and illustrator of this work
under the Copyright, Designs and Patents Act, 1988.

ISBN 1 85430 810 6

A CIP catalogue record for this book
is available from the British Library

Printed in Belgium

10 9 8 7 6 5 4 3 2 1

Hushabye Lily

Claire Freedman
John Bendall-Brunello

LITTLE TIGER PRESS

LONDON

Night-time crept over the farmyard.
The moon rose higher into the darkening sky.
  "Are you still awake, Lily?" said Mother Rabbit.
"You should be fast asleep by now."
  "I'm trying, but I can't sleep," Lily replied.
"The farmyard's far too noisy for sleeping,"
                        and she pricked up her ears.
                          "What's that quacking sound
                            I can hear?" she asked.

"Hush now!" said Mother Rabbit. "It's only the ducks, resting in the tall reeds."

"Sorry, Lily!" called out a golden-eyed duck.

"Are we keeping you awake? We were only singing
sleepy bedtime songs to one another. Would you
like me to sing you a song, too?"

"Yes, please!" Lily said.

So the duck puffed out his chest, shook out his feathers,
and sang the most beautiful duck lullaby he knew.
"That was lovely!" sighed Lily, sleepily.
"Shhh!" whispered the duck. And without a sound,
he waddled away, back to the moonlit pond.

"Tu-whit, tu-whoo!"
hooted the owl
on the barn roof.
"Hush!" whispered
Lily's mother.
The owl flew away,
high into the sky.

TU-WHIT TU-WHOO

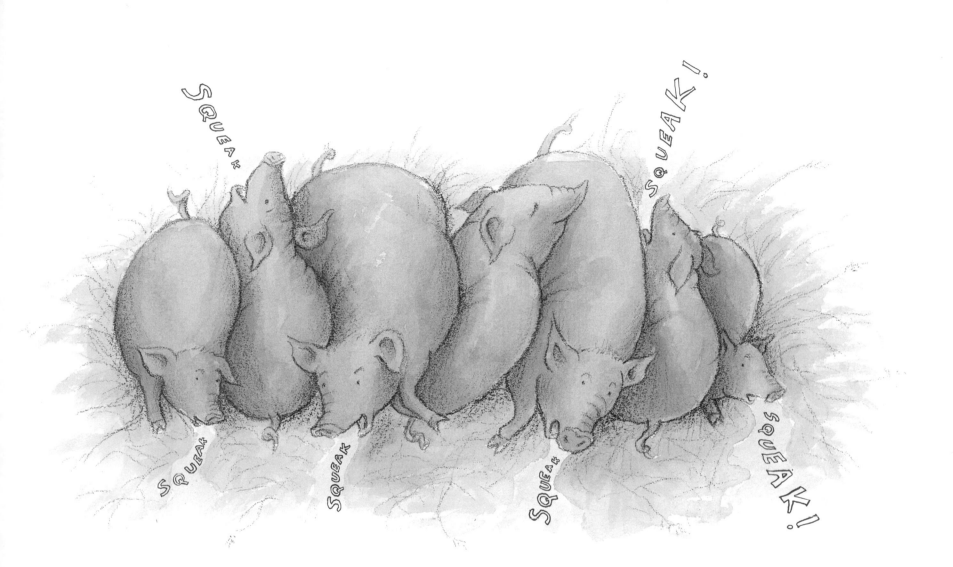

"Squeak, squeak," yawned the piglets,
nestling top-to-tail in the pigsty.
"Shhh!" sighed Mother Rabbit. "Hush!"
Sleepily, Lily closed her eyes . . .

. . . but before long she opened them again, and pricked up her ears.

"What's that moo-ing sound I can hear?" she asked.

"Hush now!" said Mother Rabbit. "It's only the cows lowing in the cowshed."

"Sorry, Lily!" cried out a soft-eyed cow. "Are we keeping you awake? We were only telling each other bedtime stories. Would you like to hear a story, too?"

"Ooh, yes please!" said Lily.

So the cow told Lily her favourite sleepy bedtime tale.
"That was nice!" said Lily with a huge yawn.
"Shhh!" whispered the cow. And she lumbered back
to the old barn, as quietly as she could.

"Miaow!" cried the farm cat,
huddling her kittens together.

MIAOW

"Hee-haw!" brayed the dreaming donkey,
turning in his sleep.

"Shhh!" sighed Lily's mother. "Hush now!"
Lily closed her eyes . . .

. . . but then she opened them again and pricked
up her ears.

"What's that clucking sound I can hear?" she asked.

"Hush!" said Mother Rabbit. "It's only the hens
hiding in the haystacks."

"Sorry, Lily!" called out a bright-eyed hen.

"Are we keeping you awake? We were only collecting straw to make our beds more comfortable. Shall I find some straw for you, too?"

"I'd like that," said Lily.

So the hen brought back a beakful of straw,
and tucked it under Lily's head.
"That's cosy," said Lily, struggling to
keep her eyes open.
"Shhh!" whispered the hen, and she
crept off softly to the hen coop, on tiptoes.

"Shhh!" hushed the ducks
to the rippling reeds.

"Shhh!" hushed the cows
to the leaves on the trees.

"Shhh!" hushed the hens
to the whispering wind.

"Hush now, Lily!" whispered Mother Rabbit,
and she snuggled up against her little one.
The moon hid behind the clouds.
All was quiet and still, until . . .

. . . down in the shadowy stable, a little brown foal
opened his eyes and pricked up his ears.
"What's that whistling sound I can hear?" he asked.
"Shhh, go back to sleep!" his mother whispered.
"It's only little Lily snoring!"